To my little Alexsaurus

Text and illustrations
copyright © 1993
by Linda Martin.
All rights reserved.
Design and calligraphy
by Laura Jane Coats.
Printed in Hong Kong.

ISBN 0-8118-0122-5
CIP Data Available.

Distributed in Canada
by Raincoast Books
112 East Third Avenue
Vancouver, B.C. V5T 1C8

10 9 8 7 6 5 4 3 2 1

Chronicle Books
275 Fifth Street
San Francisco, California
94103

When Dinosaurs Go Visiting
by Linda Martin

Chronicle Books San Francisco

When dinosaurs go visiting,
They wear their nicest clothes.
Their nicest shoes,
Their nicest shirts,
Their nicest pair of hose.

Their teeth are brushed,
Their nails are trimmed,
Their skins are shiny green.
They check each other closely,
To make sure that they are clean.

They love to bring a little gift,
And a pretty bright bouquet.
They always bring their favorite dish,
An omnivore soufflé!

They load the goodies in the car.
There's lots of room in back.

They bring a picnic lunch along
So they can stop and snack.

Then merrily they're on their way.
How fresh the morning air!
They travel many miles
Until they're finally there.

Their friends are glad to see them.
It's a very happy scene,

A house that's full of dinosaurs
So bright and shiny green.

They look at picture albums,
And they sit around and chat.
They talk about who's getting thin,
And who is growing fat.

And when they all sit down to eat,
They're never, ever rude.
They always use their napkins
And say, "Please pass the food!"

After eating ice cream
And delicious apple pie,
They all help with the dishes
Till the last one's clean and dry!

Later, they pop popcorn
And they guzzle soda pop.
They play their favorite records
And they do the dino hop!

Dancing, eating, having fun,
The time just seems to fly.
They wish they could stay longer,
But it's time to say goodbye.

There's a hug and kiss for everyone.
"We had a ball!" they say.
"But it's going to be a long drive back.
We must be on our way."

And when their visit's over,
They leave by the light of the moon.
"What a day!" they say, as they drive away.
"Hope you'll visit *us* real soon!"